THE SUN
92 MILLION

THE MOON
0.25 MIL

MERCURY
48 MILLION

VENUS
25 MILLION

MARS
56 MILLION

165 MILLION

CERES

391 MILLION

JUPITER

798 MILLION

SATURN

1,692 MILLION

URANUS

A large PART of the INSPIRATion
For this BOOK came From REPEATEDly
trying to EXPLAIN the HISTORY and
GEOGRAPHY of the NORThern IRELAND
CONFLICT - to SMART people, who
neither KNEW, not REALLY CARED
ABOUT it — OVER the DISTANCE
of AN OCEAN.

"From out there on the moon, international politics look
so petty. You want to grab a politician by the scruff of the
neck and drag him a quarter of a million miles out and say,
'Look at that …'"

— **Edgar Mitchell,** Apollo 14 astronaut, 1974

"For man, unlike any other thing organic or inorganic in
the universe, grows beyond his work, walks up the stairs
of his concepts, emerges ahead of his accomplishments."

— **John Steinbeck,** *The Grapes of Wrath*, 1939

To Harland and Mari
Future keepers of the peace
(I hope)

First published in hardback in the
United Kingdom by HarperCollins
Children's Books in 2022

HarperCollins *Children's Books* is a
division of HarperCollins*Publishers* Ltd
1 London Bridge Street, London SE1 9GF

www.harpercollins.co.uk

HarperCollins*Publishers*
1st Floor, Watermarque Building,
Ringsend Road, Dublin 4, Ireland

10 9 8 7 6 5 4 3

Text and illustrations copyright
© Oliver Jeffers 2022
Design by Rory Jeffers

ISBN: 978-0-00-855545-0

Printed and bound in the USA

**All calculations made by
astrophysicist Stephen Smartt**

Thank you
Suzanne Jeffers, Fru Czech, David Lewis,
Aaron Ruff, Gabe Benzur, Ben Cady,
Emma Miller, Philippa Jordan,
Ann-Janine Murtagh, Val Brathwaite,
Geraldine Stroud and Edge.

This book is a companion to the art installation
Our Place in Space – an epic scale model of
the solar system. The 10km sculpture trail was
developed by Oliver Jeffers, astrophysicist
Professor Stephen Smartt, and the Nerve Centre
and creative partners, as part of the UNBOXED
programme funded by the UK government.

www.ourplaceinspace.earth

MEANWHILE BACK ON EARTH...

OLIVER JEFFERS

HarperCollins *Children's Books*

In all of the cosmos...

...this one place in our solar system...

...is where all of the people have lived...

for the whole time we've been people.

We have always thought that Earth

is so big . . .

...that it's best to divide it into smaller bits.

It seems we humans...

...have always fought each other over space.

So ... if we were already at the moon,
it would be almost a year ago at home.

And we'd see Earth much as we left it
at the start of the twenty-first century

where everyone seems distracted
and can't agree what we do next.

If we took a left turn at the moon (towards the sun), it would be a
seventy-eight-year drive from Earth to Venus – our closest planet.

Meanwhile back on Earth,
seventy-eight years ago,

it was the middle of the twentieth century ...

and the whole planet was fighting –
hopefully for the last time.

Meanwhile back on Earth, 150 years ago,
it was late in the 1800s, and . . .

that stuck out into a small sea.

Back on our original course, it would be a 283-year drive to reach the sun.

(Make sure you have the air conditioning going, and your sunglasses on.)

Meanwhile back on Earth,
283 years ago, it was the middle of the 1700s

and some humans
(after sailing across an ocean and fighting with the humans who were already there)

were about to start fighting each other.

Now, if we'd made that right turn towards Mars, and kept going,
we would be driving for 500 years, from Earth, before we saw anything else.

When we eventually did, it would probably be Ceres, the largest object in the asteroid belt.

Checking in the year-view mirror,
we see that back on Earth, 500 years ago,

and the Vikings had finished fighting everyone around them,
so they built boats to find new people to fight.

But let's keep going,

as it's only a short 2,400-year drive to Saturn.

Meanwhile back on Earth, two and a half millennia ago,

some people were building the largest wall ever to be made . . .

so they could keep all the other people out.

Meanwhile back on Earth, 5,000 years ago,
people discovered using animals and metal

made fighting much more effective.

Back on Earth, it is 6,000 BCE and the
sea is still rising from the end of the last Ice Age ...

Back on Earth, 1,200 years ago,
it was the year 800 (and something),

the first people from one big bit of land
arrived at the other big bit of land and ran riot.

I hope you're comfortable (and brought snacks),
as it takes almost 1,200 years to drive to Jupiter.

after driving for 11,000 years, we finally reach Pluto.

there are fewer people on Earth than currently live in Ireland
(around six million) . . .

and early people are fighting
each other with sticks and stones.

If we carry on,

and they are much too busy surviving
to bother with fighting each other.

Well, that's us. We have reached the end of our solar system

(just one of billions).

Do you want to keep going?

(Next stop: Alpha Centauri, just a seventy-seven-million-year drive away.)

Or,

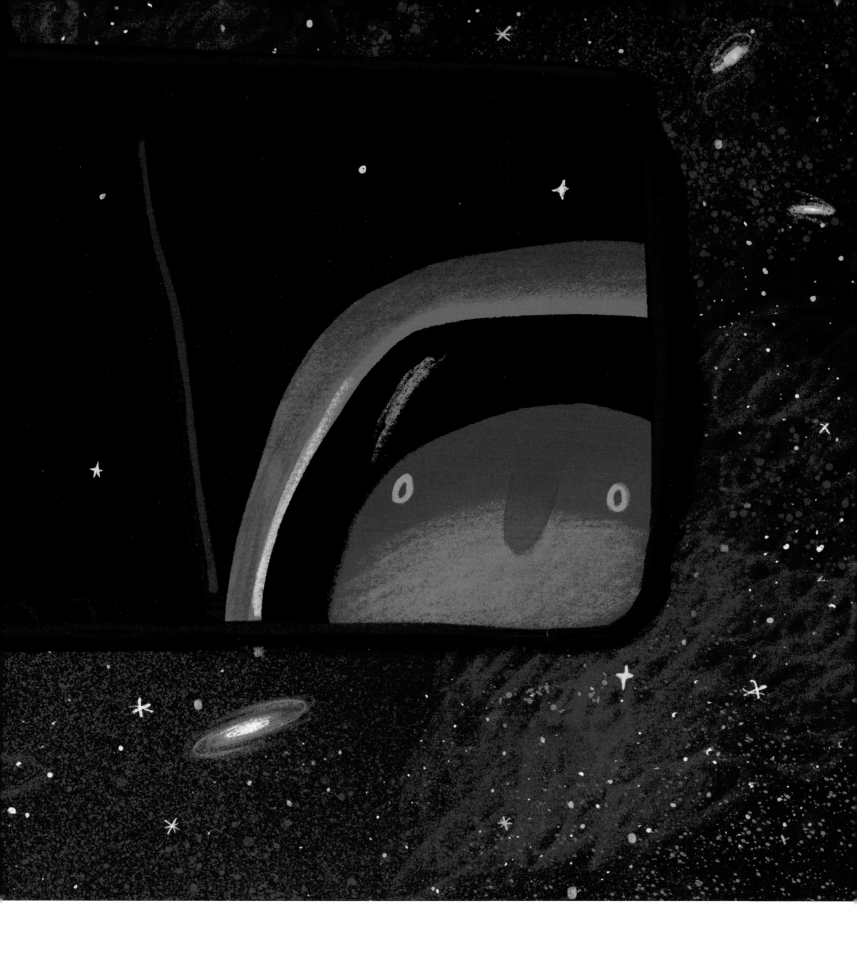

do you want to go home?

"No matter where you travel, it's always nice to get home."

— **Neil Armstrong,** on returning to Earth on Apollo 11, 1969

EARTH
TODAY

2022
-THE
BEGINNING
OF THE
FUTURE

The Moon
1 YEAR

2021
-NEWS INDUSTRY
/SOCIAL MEDIA

VENUS
78 YEARS

1939—1945
—SECOND WORLD WAR

MERCURY
150 YEARS

1880s
—EUROPEAN
COLONISATION
OF AFRICA

MARS
170 YEARS

1853—1856
—THE CRIMEAN WAR

The SUN
283 YEARS

1775—1783
—THE U.S. WAR
OF INDEPENDENCE
FROM BRITAIN, MANY
NATIVE PEOPLES DIED

CERES
500 YEARS

1519 CE
—SPANISH
CONQUEST
OF THE
AZTEC EMP

SATURN
2,400 YEARS

200—220 BCE
—CONSTRUCTION
OF THE
GREAT WALL OF CHINA

URANUS
5,000 YEARS

3,000 BCE — BRONZE AGE
—ANCIENT BABYLONIANS and ANCIENT EGYPTIANS
(ALTHOUGH THEY NEVER FOUGHT EACH OTHER
THEY BOTH MASTERED THE USE OF BRONZE
AND HORSES IN WARFARE)

TIME
From EARTH
*at 37 mph

Though, really, Earth is not so big. Not compared to . . .

it will take almost a year to drive there.

(All speeds and distances calculated at 37mph* – the average speed humans drive at.)

*miles per hour

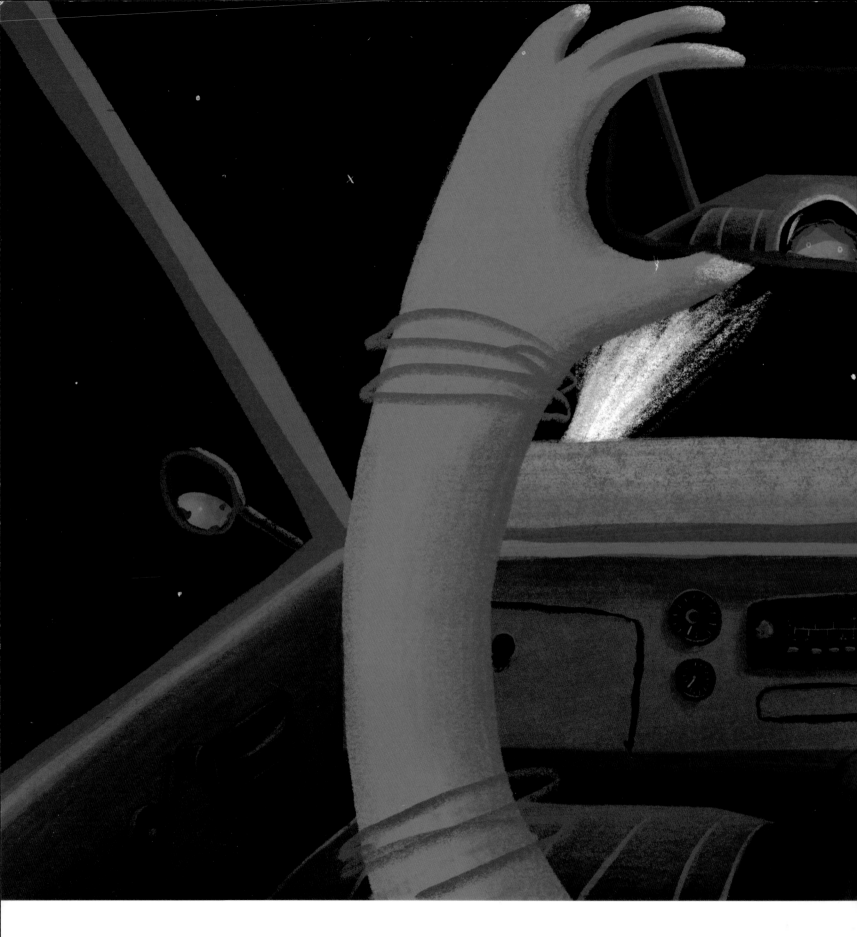

On this trip it's important to keep checking the mirror
to see what we're up to back on Earth.

well, SPACE.

Shall we take a detour and see for ourselves?

Then, let's put on our space helmets...

turn this into a space car ...

...and head out towards the moon.
It is a quarter of a million miles away so